Anonymous

Twilight dreams

Being poems and pictures of life and nature

Anonymous

Twilight dreams
Being poems and pictures of life and nature

ISBN/EAN: 9783337269579

Printed in Europe, USA, Canada, Australia, Japan

Cover: Foto ©Andreas Hilbeck / pixelio.de

More available books at **www.hansebooks.com**

"LET ME, THEN, THY TRUE LOVE BE."

BEING

Poems and Pictures of Life and Nature

ILLUSTRATIONS BY

FRED BARNARD.
ROBERT BARNES.
ALLAN BARRAUD.
W. H. J. BOOT.
GEORGE CLAUSEN.
FRANK DADD.
FRANK DICKSEE, A.R.A.

M. ELLEN EDWARDS.
W. BISCOMBE GARDNER.
MARY L. GOW.
CHARLES GREGORY.
W. HATHERELL.
ARTHUR HOPKINS.
G. G. KILBURNE.

R. W. MACBETH, A.R.A.
W. H. OVEREND.
SUTTON PALMER.
J. McL. RALSTON.
WILLIAM SMALL.
W. L. WYLLIE.
&c. &c.

NEW YORK

CASSELL PUBLISHING COMPANY

104 & 106 Fourth Avenue

CONTENTS.

Contents—*Continued.*

"MY Margaret, would that I could be
    The breeze which softly kisses thee;
Or else those sunbeams, warm and bright,
Which crown thy head with golden light."
"The breeze," she answered, "dies away,
And sunbeams fade with close of day."

"Then if I were those flowers fair
Which thou, dear girl, art carrying there,
To wear perchance upon thy breast—
Oh, happy flowers, so loved, so blest !"
"The flowers fair must fade," said she ;
"Then I shall cast them off from me :"

"Well, let me then thy true love be,
Winning thine every thought for me ;
I'll envy not the breeze or flower,
Nor e'en the sunshine's golden dower."
"Ah, *love* I cannot cast away,
But hold for ever, night and day !"

Mary D. Brine.

7

A LETTER.

GOOD news or evil, sunshine or shadow—
  What is the message the postman bore,
Meeting a lassie midway in the meadow,
  Bringing a letter from distant shore?
" Wounded to death ! "—so ran the letter—
  " Wounded to death in the front of the fray ! "
Dying right nobly surely is better
  Than living to bask in life's sunniest ray !

" Wounded to death ! "—Ay. *almost* to dying,
  But the great God gave back the life that seemed lost,
And even now while the maiden was sighing,
  The far-stretching leagues of the ocean were crossed.
And just when the sky seemed most cloudy and dreary,
  And all was as dark as a dull autumn day,
The soldier was back with his own little dearie,
  And the sunshine burst forth with a glad summer ray.

David Frane

8

FAREWELL TO THE SWALLOWS.

MUST you go, and leave us
    lone,
        Companions of our summer
            hours?
Alas! when you afar have flown
    A weary life will then be ours.
We oft have watched at sunny eve
    The changes in your airy flight,
And longed like you the air to cleave
    With hearts all buoyant with delight.

We saw you come in lovely spring,
    When all the earth was bright and gay,
And hearty was our welcoming,
    Yet you so soon will fly away!
To southern lands, where spring is still,
    And balmy odours fill the air,

You haste o'er stream and dale and hill:
    O would that we could follow there!

With you depart sweet summer days,
    And winter shows its icy hand;
Bright flow'rets fade before our gaze,
    And falling leaves bestrew the land.
Ah, you must go, alas! farewell!
    'Twere death for you with us to stay,
But hopes within our hearts will dwell
    That we shall meet again in May.
                EDWARD OXENFORD.

9

THE VILLAGE MAY-DAY.

PILED up with sacks, to yonder town
The great mill-waggon lumbers down;
Drawn by three horses, tall and strong,
The great mill-waggon rolls along.

The miller's smock is clean and new,
And smart with ribbons, red and blue;
And tinkling bells on bridle-rein
Have made the stately horses vain.

And every year the first of May
Is made the village holiday:
The school is closed: the children run
In meadows smiling with the sun.

And now before the mill they wait,
While some, impatient, climb the gate,
And shout with glee, when drawing near
The loudly rumbling wheels they hear.

And soon the horses loom in sight,
With gay rosettes and harness bright,
While close beside the leader's head
The miller walks with sturdy tread.

Long may the festive day come round
And find the miller hale and sound,
And may his goods increase, and still
The great wheel turn his busy mill.

J. R. EASTWOOD.

THE SISTERS' CHOICE: A SONNET.

"HE whom I love," cries sunny thought-
less Rose,
"Must be a hero, dauntless in the
fight,
Fair as Apollo, gifted with the might
Of Ajax, triumphing where'er he goes."
Madge looks up from her book with face that
glows:
"He rather shall be precious in my sight
Who has the strength to choose and do the
right,
Who's kind and gentle both to friends and
foes."

So speak the sisters, each as she deems
best,
Each with a bright ideal of her own:
Yet who can tell what lot to each may
fall?
Love is a kindly master after all,
And buries the ideals we have known,
That present bliss may bring us joy and rest.

G. WEATHERLY.

UNTRODDEN.

WHAT have we here?
Immensity, and power, and solitude.
The bristling crags spread out in rugged might,
The torrent dashes down, resistless, vast,
Suggestive of illimitable lakes
Or boundless plains of sun-kissed, melting snow.
The grandest forest-tree is here a dwarf
Beside that giant, hoar with froth and foam.
The clouds are big with thunder: no less voice
Could answer back the cataract's loud roar.
This is no home for puny things called men;
They would destroy its grandeur—utilise
That stream magnificent—quarry the crags—
Blot Nature's name from this her fairest page.
It is too great for man; 'tis fit for God—
And God alone dwells here!

I. B.

WHAT THE RIVER SAYETH.

"I HAVE rushed thro' the rocks with a wild-foaming roar,
    But now, like a traveller, weary—
  Whose life is troubled, whose heart is sore
  And whose future is darkly dreary—
I rest 'neath the pleasant soft shade of the trees
  In the depths of Reflection's calm pool,
And gather fresh strength from a moment of ease
  And my feverish hurryings cool.

I was born in the Cloud-land, endowed with swift motion,
    And sent on my mission through Earth
To bear onward men's thoughts, like their ships, to the
      ocean,
    There to find in that death their true birth;
'Tis for this that my powers are ceaselessly hurled
    'Gainst obstructions of dull rock and shoal,
To contribute pure waters to freshen the world
    And to gladden the sorrowful soul.

WM. A. GIBBS.

13

SPRING BLOSSOMS.

THERE is no time so sweet as spring,
  When Nature dons her best ;
Dispell'd is gloom when bud and bloom
  Awake from winter's rest.

The birds again their carols sing
  Within the vernal trees ;
And violets rise, with purple eyes,
  To greet the gentle breeze !

  O spring is sweet, for ev'ry flow'r
    Glows gaily in the sun ;
  And in the air it breathes a pray'r
    For hours so sweet begun !

No longer reigns the frost and snow,
  Soft summer now is nigh ;
The buds of spring the tidings bring
  That wintry days must die ;

O'er hill and dale the herald roves,
  With flow'rets in his hand,
And casts away the blossoms gay
  To deck the waking land !

  O spring is sweet, for ev'ry flow'r
    Glows gaily in the sun ;
  And in the air it breathes a pray'r
    For hours so sweet begun !

EDWARD OXENFORD.

14

On the Bridge where the Rivers meet.

YEARS ago, when the wind was low,
    And the east was dim and grey,
      And the west was red with the sunset-glow,
And the daylight ebbed away.
And never a sound came through the night
    Save the rush of waters fleet,
I stood where I stand in the waning light,
    On the bridge where the rivers meet.

To the north the tall tors kissed the sky,
    To the south was the restful sea,
To the right and left green hills rose high,
    And a high hill fronted me ;
And down twin valleys on either hand
    Raced the streams to meet and greet,
As I stood in the dusk where now I stand,
    On the bridge where the rivers meet.

Over the river from left to right
    Spread a mist across the vale,
Like a still sea, spectral, filmy, and white ;
    And the crescent moon rose pale.
And the stars looked down on the streams that sped
    Through the arches 'neath my feet,
As I stood where I stand, with drooping head,
    On the bridge where the rivers meet.

The years have come, and the years have gone,
    And have left their marks on me ;
But the river unchanged speeds gaily on
    To the ever-changing sea ;
The hills are unaltered far and near,
    And the still scene is complete ;
I alone seem changed who linger here
    On the bridge where the rivers meet.

CHARLES JOHNS.

15

A DAY DREAM

IT fell upon a day in Summertide,
   When leaves were densest, and a gloom of shade
   Sank deepest down upon the woodland glade,
    And all the birds were mute—I lay beside
A lake within the forest's heart; and lo!
   Lulled by the heat, half sleeping, half awake,
   I saw, or dreamed I saw, within the lake
Strange shadowy phantoms moving to and fro.

And, floating on the surface, bubbles bright
   And many-hued were dancing—ruby-red,
   Purple and azure, and of every shade
That Iris steals from sunshine when the light
Pierces the rain-drops. Ever and anon
   I saw the phantom-creatures spring to snatch
   Some glittering bubble, and at last to catch
An airy globe that burst—and then 't was gone.

And down the creatures fell, or, thrust aside
   By others struggling upwards, passed from sight:
   And some, before they reached the water's height
Where played these mocking globules, sank and died.
While now and then I saw some creature lie
   Calm and unmoving, though before its eyes
   On the translucent water glowed a prize
Brightest and largest, dancing vainly by.

While thus I gazed upon this wondrous scene,
  My thoughts took shape in words, and then I cried
  Unto the forest-deeps. They only sighed
With rustling leaves, nor told what it might mean;
When, startling the deep silence, on the air
  A voice as of an Angel, sharp and clear,
  Rose cheerily from out the greensward near
And to my sense this vision did declare :—

" Man, what thou seest, is the type of life,
  And all those creatures are thy fellow men,
  Evermore vainly seeking to attain
Those bubble-prizes amid toil and strife—
Power and wealth and fame. Yet some, more wise,
  Know they are vanity and empty air,
  And so they heed them not, and give no care
To gain the glittering things the others prize.

" Soon all those little lives shall pass away,
  And all those bubbles burst. Then, mortal, know
  The nothingness of all things here below.
Elsewhere the Real seek." From where I lay
I sprang affrighted, and I looked around,
  I saw the fishes swimming in the lake,
  Darting up swift the summer flies to take,
And heard the grasshopper's clear ringing sound.
                    JOHN FRANCIS WALLER.

EARLY FLOWERS.

SWEET Spring-time flowers, from the moist earth
  peeping,
  Welcome, as sunshine after pleasant rain!
 Out of warm bulbs, that long have held you sleeping
  Like buried hopes, you start to life again.
 Welcome! and cluster on the brow of Morning;
  The icicles have melted from her hair;
 Her floating auburn tresses want adorning,
  And your pure bells shall make them very fair.

 Old Winter, crowned with mistletoe and holly,
  Is stealing from us quietly at last;
 And now the trees bud, it is worse than folly
  To muse among the ashes of the past.
 Blackbird and thrush and ouzel, in their gladness,
  Have charmed away the winter of the soul;
 The mask has fallen from ungenial sadness,
  And the benighted heart is once more whole.

 One redbreast on my window-sill yet lingers,
  And peers about with prying round black eye,
 Far cheerier than when Winter's numbing
  fingers
  Half robbed his little throat of melody;
 We cannot hearken to the ghostly voices
  Of vanished hours, and brood by lonely fires,
 Since every bursting bud and leaf rejoices,
  The faintest echo of sad sound expires.

       JANE DIXON.

Coming Home

FROM afar across the ocean,
  Homeward speeds my sailor dear—
Not in vain my long devotion,
  For at last he's sailing near !
Years have vanished since he left me,
  Gazing sadly o'er the sea ;
Oh, his bark of all bereft me—
  Now he's coming home to me !
    Farewell sorrow ! sighs are dying ;
      Tears are strangers now to me !
    For my faithful love is hieing
      Homeward o'er the smiling sea !

Where the wavelets, white and curling,
  Round the olden jetty play,—
'Neath the sea-birds airy whirling—
  I have watched from day to day !
Thoughts have risen whilst I lonely
  Pac'd along the beaten shore,
Thoughts that he, whom I love only,
  Home was coming never more !
    Farewell sorrow ! sighs are dying ;
      Tears are strangers now to me !
    For my faithful love is hieing
      Homeward o'er the smiling sea !

THE REASON.

WHAT is it gives my darling grace,
And makes her peerless in mine eyes?
Is it the glory of her face,
The myriad beauties all can trace
In her, my prize?

Is it the sunshine of her glance?
Is it the pureness of her brow?
Is it the sunny smiles that dance
On rosy lips, that so entrance
And chain me now?

No! Herein lies my darling's might;
And this is all her witchery—
That with a love that's pure and bright,
Fervent and strong as noonday light,
My love loves me!

LIFE-FURROWS: A SONNET.

TWO horses, harnessed to a plough, stand still,
   Waiting the voice whose words they've learned
    to know :
  Then, at the ploughman's signal, proudly slow
They plod with patient footsteps up the hill ;
And since with sturdy hand and steady will
  The keen-edged share is driven to and fro,
 U'p-hill and down alike the furrows go

True as a line, unturned by any ill.
Are not our lives just like the ploughman's share ?
  The Providence that rules them may decree
   That we plough up the hill through toilsome
    days,
And obstacles may meet us everywhere ;
  Yet if our hands be true in all our ways,
  The furrows will be straight and fair to see.

G. WEATHERLY.

SWEETLY ARE THE WILD BIRDS SINGING.

SWEETLY are the wild birds singing,
  Softly purls the silvery rill,
Yet though all around is lovely,
  I am lonely, lonely still !
Vainly sunbeams spread before me,
  Vainly flowers their scents impart—
I am lonely, desolation
  Reigns supreme within my heart !
    Vainly are the wild birds singing,
    Vainly purls the silv'ry rill ;
    For though all around is lovely,
    I am lonely, lonely still.

Ah ! how long ere patient waiting,
  Waiting that to bear is hard,
Finds in love that cannot alter,
  Bliss that is a full reward.
Soon, ay soon, or life will vanish,
  Hope on wearied wings depart ;
Soon, or else despair will silence
  Beatings of this weary heart !
    Vainly are the wild birds singing,
    Vainly purls the silv'ry rill ;
    For though all around is lovely,
    I am lonely, lonely still.

23

"Once Amid the Roses."

A SONG OF LOVE AND GRIEF.

ONCE amid the roses bright,
 Ruby-red, honey-sweet.
You and I, in laughing weather,
Sang a lay of love together ;
 Petals falling on our feet.
When shall summer be so light ?
  Never more !
  Oh, never more !

Once beside the snow-drops, dear,
 Waxen pale, wintry cold,
Grief and I, in wailing weather,
Sang a dirge of tears together ;
 Raindrops dripping on the mould.
When shall winter be so drear ?
  Never more !
  Ah, never more !

JANE DIXON.

LOOK in mine eyes, my fairest,
　As I look into thine ;
　　Say, is the love thou bearest
As deep and true as mine :—
Deep as the sea unfathomed,
　True as the clinging vine ?

Ah ! in thy hand no trembling
　To meet my clasp I feel ;
True faith hath no dissembling,
　True love is strong as steel !
I'll hold this hand for ever
　Through life, come woe or weal.

Aye, in these orbs clear-beaming,
　Serene, and soft, and blue,
Like stars in still lakes gleaming,
　Mine, imaged there, I view,
And know the love thou feelest
For me is deep and true.

Lay now thy hand, my dearest,
　In mine, and as thou dost,
Say. if in aught thou fearest
　On my right hand to trust,
Leaning on man securely,
　As woman ever must.

Enough.　No other token
　I ask thy faith to prove,
I want no words low-spoken
　To tell me thou dost love—
The eye and touch have language
　Though lip or tongue ne'er move.

Now, let me draw thee nearer,
　And breathe my heart's delight,
Whispering that thou art dearer
　To me than life or light,
In words as soft as breathings
　Of air in leaves at night.

J. F. WALLER.

NATURE'S COLOURS.

WHO dares to picture Nature's varying hue—
    The flashing colours of the waterfall,
    The ripening fruit upon the lichened wall,
The summer sky with all its wealth of blue,
The sunset or the storm--This must he do ;
    Let Truth to him be all, and all in all,
Since Art *must* fail unless its art be true.

A SKETCH.

AN isle of trees full foliaged in a meadow,
    Along whose quiet grassy shores below,
The glad fawns bathe in level lengths of shadow;
And sweet airs, amiable as summer, blow
Warmly and faint among the happy leaves,
Loving each other in a green repose
Folded, or waking in the slumb'rous glow,
Where the wind passing indolently weaves
A net of lazy listless whisperings,
Most like the liquid lullaby of spring's,
Pulsing demure and quaintly in some cool
Dell of the woods, unseen, save of some ray
Piercing the boughs, having somewhat to say
To fairies couched on bubbles round the pool.

                                    T. C. IRWIN.

SUMMER DAYS

O H, blessed summer days of long
        ago!
    Your vision makes a sunshine in the
        shade,
  That mystic sunshine that need never fade,
Though life may send us tempests, frosts, and
    snow,
So let us take all bliss we find below,
    For half the future from the past is
    made;

And every happy hour in store is laid,
    To make us richer as we older grow.
  Nay, when I dream of the green woodland
    lane
  Beside the churchyard where my darling lies,
I stint my tears, lest even softest rain
  Ruffle the lake that mirrors sun lit skies;
  For Hope best knows the heaven she longs to
    gain,
  By sweetest page in memory's treasuries.

M

TOGETHER.

 A SAPLING oak, with clinging ivy bound,
    So that in common, on their leaves en-
       twined,
  The warm sun shines, or blows the wintry wind ;
Together both grow upward, and are crowned
With all the glory in perfection found,
    And then together in old age decay,
    Until at last there comes a stormy day,
That bears them, still twined closely, to tne ground.

Two loving hearts, finn-bound in early youth,
    That pass together down the vale of years,
      Through sunny joys, through cloudy griefs and
        fears,
So closely knit in bonds of love and truth,
That when old age comes on, still hand in hand,
They both pass onward to the Better Land.

                G. WEATHERLY.

A NOON-DREAM.

TWAS in a noon-dream by the summer bay,
    Spirit, thy vision rose upon my sight ;
  A presence which came floating o'er the spray
  Like a rich soul of odorous wind and light,
That seemed familiar as one passed away,
  Gentle, beloved, returned from yonder height
To guard and to inspire ; and all that day
Most radiant phantasies, aërial, warm,
And sweet as summer, vibrating at will,
My fancy shaped : nor art thou gone, for still
  I dream of thee when sorrow and when night
Are round me, and my fancy shapes thy form,
  And brow of meteor-beauty, that on me
  Glows from the levels of the star-dim sea

30

AUTUMN.

BEYOND the mountains sloped in gloomy
    grey,
  A ruined continent of golden cloud,
  Blown seaward on the wind of sunset, showed
  Beneath its fiery toppling summits proud,
The shapes of flaming cities stretched away,
    With amphitheatre and obelisk
  Above the murmurous sea's saturnine disk,
Awhile : until, distombed in stormy glare,
It streamed in ashen islands down the air ;
    Then up the void the wind dolorous heaves
The dark battalions of the clouds, and bodes
  Over the glooming lands where twilight grieves.
Inconstant ; drifting o'er the sad dry roads,
  Monotonous litanies of withered leaves.

31

A BRIDAL SONG.

DOST thou linger, gentle maiden,
　At the minster door?
Dost thou tremble, tender maiden,
　On the chancel floor?
Dost thou fear, and dost thou falter,
　When thou kneelest at the altar?
With the bridegroom by thee now
Wilt thou take the marriage vow?

If thy heart, O loving maiden!
　Thou hast given away,
Without fear, O trustful maiden!
　Give thy hand to-day.

Leaving father, leaving mother,
Give thy life unto another,
Taking back a dearer life
From his love as wedded wife.

Let him lead thee, wedded maiden,
　From the altar now.
Thou art his for ever, maiden,
　By that marriage vow.
His in joy and sorrow ever,
None these holy bonds may sever.
Loving, trusting, stand beside
Him who loves thee, happy bride!
　　　　　　　J. F. WALLER.

AT AN ITALIAN SPINNING-WHEEL.

RUN, my wheel, run fast and faster! Love will
　laugh at all disaster;
　　What if Beppo see Lucia near the pine-grove
　　on the hill?
Honeyed words and fair pretences may beguile his
　wandering senses,
　But the finch once more his mate seeks when the
　fowler's pipe is still.

Run, my wheel, run fast and faster! Say, hath love
　then found its master,
　That my heart is vaguely throbbing, and my glances
　seek the gate?
And at length when sunset flushes all the west, my
　cheeks with blushes
　Are aflame because a step comes—but the vineyard-
　dresser, late!

Run, my wheel, now slow, more slowly! Do these
　knots, the white wool wholly
　Complicating, weave in tangles till e'en patience
　half despairs?
Sadly now bodes sober reason that in time a chilly
　season
　Sorrow-laden must succeed ere use love's plighted
　circle wears.

Run, my wheel, run slow, more slowly! Let e'en
　happiness be lowly,
　And remember how the future days of darkness will
　disclose;

Yet my blackbird "tirra lirra" sings; and when I ask
　my mirror,
　Beauty whispers, loving trust and hope disarm love's
　ancient foes.

Stop, my wheel! Ah! threads, by breaking you
　remind me that forsaking
　Snaps a life-love more than death parts; I'll address
　me to my wool;
Love and Duty are twin-sisters, with them walk we
　through the vistas
　Of the darkened days in front, and trust with
　mercies they'll be full.

Run, my wheel, again, run gaily! Jealous angers, die
　out daily!
　Can Lucia's eyes dim these? her love, what is it
　matched with mine?
Round her face my moth may flutter, but should trouble
　even mutter
　Near my heart, he'd swift fly back with "Giulietta!
　I am thine!"

Run, my wheel—but why this trembling? Peace, my
　heart, no more dissembling!
　Some one comes—the blackbird chirrups—still
　advances—still alarms—
Through the oleanders pushes—by the roses careless
　brushes—
　Stop, my wheel—ah, stop!—'tis Beppo! and I'm
　locked within his arms!　　M. G. WATKINS.

THE MAYFLOWER AT NEW PLYMOUTH

THE CHURCH OF THE PILGRIM FATHERS.

BY ISABELLA BANKS.

TO the green primeval forests across the
western wave,
    Oppression drove a slender band of
    true hearts strong and brave :
They could not think as others thought, nor
feel as others felt,
Nor obey the royal edict to kneel where
others knelt ;
But they had heard of shores afar by priestly
feet untrod ;
So they sought that land for conscience'
sake -- their
guiding star,
their God !

No gallant bark was theirs to steer, only a
time-worn boat,
With stores as small as seamanship—and
yet she kept afloat,
For Faith and Hope were at the helm amid
the tempest's roar ;—
But Hope was dead and Faith was numb
before they reached the shore,
Where children faint, and
women pale, first pressed
their feeble feet,
And stretched out hungry
hands to clasp their last
few grains of wheat.

Five grains of wheat!—ay, think of it!—were all
  for each thin hand,
When the Mayflower had sailed her last, and brought
  her freight to land.
But—for prayer and praise unfettered, at once the
  welkin rang

And they, who from cathedral aisles had fled in fear
  and scorn,
In a grander God-built temple could worship eve and
  morn,
Beneath the interlacing boughs like arches overhead,

With the anthems of thanksgiving those grateful
  pilgrims sang,
Ere a roof was theirs to shelter, or fruits their
  parched lips prest—
They had touched the land of promise, and left to
  God the rest!

Where verdure of a virgin turf a silent carpet
  spread,
And stately as a pillared shaft uprose each tall tree-
  bole,
With the sun-rays—God's bright fingers—to glorify
  the whole.

TO A REDBREAST

SWEET bird, a story saith thy breast
    Turned red when in Gethsemane
        Thrice, from a bleeding soul, Christ prayed:
And since that, thou hast loved to be
The most where sorrow dwells, and shade :
O'er fallen leaves, that chide the wind ;
Or near some door with cloud behind
To sing of light—to sing of rest.

E. G. CHARLESWORTH.

THE FELLING OF THE TREES.

IN the groves, where birds are singing,
  Loud the woodman's axe is ringing,
  And the trees are falling, falling,
     Like dead monarchs to the ground ;
And the tree-tops, softly sighing,

In the world to which we're clinging
Don't we hear the axe too ringing,
While the sons of toil are falling
     In whole forests to the ground?
And the souls of men are sighing,

Chant sad dirges for the dying,
And the breezes low replying
  Seem to whisper all around :
"'Tis the common fate they're meeting,
Soon or late will come the greeting
  Of the woodman unto all !
Some with gaunt arms grim and olden ;
Some with proud boughs ivy-folden ;
Some with young-year leafage golden,
     Straight and tall !
Some with props and stays upholden,
     Lest they fall !

Murm'ring dirges for the dying,
While all brave hearts are replying.
  Looking past the grassy mound :
"'Tis the common lot we're meeting,
Soon or late must come the greeting
  Of the Woodman Death to all !
Some whom Time has passed o'er lightly !
Some whose chubby hands clasp nightly !
Some whose sad eyes light up brightly
     At the call !
Some whose sparse locks glimmer whitely !
     All must fall !"

G. WEATHERLY.

37

SONG OF THE MORNING.

LIGHT from beyond the sea up-breaking
Whitens the stainless blue afar ;
Pale in heaven is the morning star ;
Earth from the hush of sleep is waking.

Glowing clouds on the glowing azure,
Amber and rose, with golden rim,
Over the far horizon dim,
Sailing away in light-winged measure.

Waves and waves on the dusky ocean
Flash and burn in the rising light,
Numberless, wide as the infinite,
Mingle and blend in bright commotion.

Drops of light on the branches quiver,
Drops of light on the grasses gleam,
Pure and clear as the morning beam,
Shake and shine by the shining river.

Clad in light, and the low winds shaking
Dews from her beautiful locks, earth lies
Smiling up to the beautiful skies—
Earth from the hush of sleep is waking.

JOHN HUIE.

38

THE BELLS AND THE WAVES.

THE Waves.—What is your song, O bells?
  The Bells.—We ring to rest, to praise, and
      prayer;
          God's hand and love are everywhere.
The Waves.—Ring on, O bells, and bless the twilight
      air,
      We, too, are God's, for he is every-
          where.

The Bells.—What is your song, O waves?
The Waves.—Sunshine and storm, no rest have we,
      Our song is of eternity.
The Bells.—Eternity! eternity!
The Poet.—The bells shall ring, the waves shall chime,
      Through all the years of deepening time,
      Till time itself at last shall be
      Merged in God's chime—eternity.

FREDERICK E. WEATHERLY.

THE RUSTIC STILE.

I KNOW a wood, far, far away—
  There was a rustic stile,
By which I've stayed at close of day,
  To rest and think awhile.
From there I've watched the setting sun
  Trail down the western sky,
Or heard the breeze, when night begun,
  Among the branches sigh.

And many stayed beside that stile
  Who did not care for trees,
Nor yet the passing time to while
  With setting sun or breeze.
Yet though, perhaps, they have forgot
  Its every sight and sound,
They'll call it still the dearest spot
  In all the world around.

The shady trees are cut away,
  And all the leaves are brown,
The lovers have grown old and grey,
  The stile has crumbled down,
To many a heart the days long flown
  Have made the place a shrine ;
And thought of happy days I've known
  Have made it one to mine.

                                    REA.

THE FISHER-GIRL'S SONG.

BY THE REV. M. G. WATKINS.

FLY, my needle, through the drift-
net, while love sings an evening
song ;
Love can lighten every burden, with
love's aid no toil is long.

Far at sea's my fisher-laddie, but there's
sunshine on the deep ;
Love misgives, though, darksome night
falls ; in its arms care cannot sleep.

Grimly smiles the fort this evening ; by
its guns the sea-pinks bloom ;
With the morning through grey mist-
wreaths death in thund'rous foam
may boom.

Many a gallant ship sails outward bound,
and never home comes more,
Or, returning home in safety, goes to
pieces on the shore.

Ocean's heart is deeply bosomed, but its
face is seamed with scars ;
Fair of promise, love's beginnings, sunken
isles, then reefs and bars.

On the rocks rue's glory rests, and swaying weeds their sternness deck ;
Cruel rocks aye in their strength ; see !
yonder by them lies a wreck.

Fly, my needle, through the gashes where
    the seals their inroads made ;
Toil is long when love is absent, by a kiss
    is toil repaid.

Oh, come sunshine, darkness, death, or
    wreck or ruin, give me love !
Love can heal all ills here, Hope says ;
    and Faith whispers, " Up above !"

TO THE RESCUE.

A MID thick mists of freezing blinding spray,
    Sad-hearted watchers on the rocky shore
      Hear the ship signals 'mid the tempest's roar :
" No boat can live in such a sea," they say ;
" Who tries to save must cast his life away !"
    And yet brave crews speed gladly to the fore,
    And bring the wreck'd ones back to life once more,
Empower'd by Him Whom winds and waves obey.

So is it ever here : Man, proudly wise,
    Cries, " Hope is lost ; in vain to work or pray !"
Then He, in Whom the highest mercy lies,
    Looks down from heaven in loving gracious way,
And man himself is strengthened to do well
By Him to whom all things are possible.

SAVING HANDS.

WHEN men need help, can we pass coldly by?
　　When, with despairing hearts, the
　　　　mourners weep,
　Dare we, unmoved, sink tranquilly to sleep?
Have we no ears to hear the widow's sigh—
The wife's lament—the hopeless bitter cry
　That reaches us across the troubled deep,
　When the fierce waves their awful harvest reap,
And one by one brave hearts sink down and die?
Has Pity lost her old-time loving touch?
　Does Charity but seek herself to please?
　　Nay, God be praised, kind hearts will ever be
To whom Christ's words are spoken : " Inasmuch
　As ye have done it unto one of these,
　　Ye have most truly done it unto Me."

　　　　　　　　　　　　　　　G. W.

DEPARTED DAYS.

SUMMER'S sweet breath, and winter's wind,
　　Have swept the landscape since I stood
　　And watch'd the ebbing of the flood,
And knew the anguish of a mind

That in wild ebb and flow was tost,
　　When, as the leaves of autumn fell,

When all the music overhead
Was but the echo of our own.

Proud loom the distant towers ; the moon
　　Sheds its pale splendours over all ;
　　While night, with tender, noiseless pall,
Hath cover'd earth and me too soon.

Upon my spirit came the knell
That she would with the flowers be lost.

A gleam of hope, like that rich light
　　Which gives October golden bloom,
　　Rose in my breast, but set in gloom :
'Twas but sun dying into night.

Now she is gone, and I alone
　　Have trod the paths we used to tread,

O long-lost moments ! nevermore
　　Shall ye return, or I leap up
　　To drink from that divinest cup
My lips once drank from, o'er and o'er

Adieu, ye glades of Paradise !
　　For such, in sooth, ye were to me ;
　　I go where I would ever be—
To kiss the grave wherein she lies.

THE RAINBOW'S SECRET.

THE sky is dark with sullen clouds:
    The fields are sad with rain;
    When breaks a light behind the hills
      And shines upon the plain,
And eyes that seldom look above
    Are lifted up on high,
With hope's old heart-beats to behold
    A rainbow in the sky.

A relic of less doubting days—
    In childhood we were told,

That where the rainbow touched the earth
    There lay a key of gold;
And if one reached the radiant spot,
    To him it should be given
To find the key which would unlock
    The very gate of heaven.

Heaven touches earth on every side,
    We say—and this to see!
Where'er we stand the rainbow rests,
    And we have found the key.

ISA CRAIG.

LIZZIE

NOW that poor Lizzie's dead,
　　It's not the same place ;
　We're all as dull as lead,
　　　For want of her face—
We sit all day and stitch
For the gay and for the rich,
But the workshop seems so dreary,
And our stitching makes us weary,
　And no laughing jest is told,
　　　　Now Lizzie's cold !

Poor Liz ! she'd lovely eyes,
　They were large and bright,
And beamed like two blue skies
　With a tender light.
And her hair was fine as silk,
And her teeth as white as milk,
And her pleasant merry laughter
Woke the room from floor to rafter—
　But all this *does* seem so old
　　　　Now Lizzie's cold !

She used to keep us girls
　In a constant grin ;
Why, a shake of her curls
　Would make us begin.
And when Madam's back was turned,
How she brightened, flushed and burned,
As she slipped on with a titter
Some fine dress that wouldn't fit her,
　'Midst our laughter loud and bold—
　　　　And now she's cold !

She'd a wonderful art
　Of mimicking too,
And there wasn't a part
　That Liz couldn't do.
If she chanced to hear the play,
We were sure to have next day
A treat of the things she'd seen there,
Just as good as though we'd been there,
　So well was her story told—
　　　　And now she's cold !

Old Madam stiff and prim,
　And as hard as flint :
Her face grown pinched and grim,
　With scraping and stint—
Even she would sometimes thaw
At the merry sights she saw ;
For poor Lizzie was endearing,
And her ways were soft and cheering,
　In the pleasant days of old,
　　　　Ere she grew cold !

The whole time she was here,
　Not a harsh word passed ;
She was our petted dear
　Up to the last.
For it's sweet to be with one
Who is bright and full of fun ;
Most girls are so uninviting,
So jealous, and so backbiting,
　But Liz was as good as gold—
　　　　And now she's cold !

For she was weak and slight,
　With a delicate chest ;
Her cough grew worse each night,
　And gave her no rest ;
And the cruel winter sleet,
Pouring down upon the street,
With its grip of iron shook her—
Till the angels came and took her
　To their peaceful distant fold,
　　　　And she grew cold !

Yes, now poor Lizzie's dead
　It's not the same place ;
We're all as dull as lead
　For want of her face.
But as we sit and stitch,
For the gay and for the rich,
There resounds an angels' chorus,
And rising in grace before us
　Sweet Liz comes as of old,
　　　　No longer cold !
　　　　　REGINALD BARNETT.

SLEEP!

SLEEP! Sleep!
   Sleep, my dearie, sleep, and dream!
    Roaming where roses are rife,
To sweeten the tear-fed stream
   That waters the tree of life ;
Take thou my song for a boat,
   And sail on my voice for a sea ;
There let it wander, and float
   Where thou desirest to be.

An thou fearest, lift thine eyes,
   For mine are thy guiding star
To light thee where heaven lies

Behind yon fiery bar.
There laughing and clapping of hands,
   Bright angels with shining feet
Run over the golden sand
   To greet thee, and meet thee, my sweet.

   Sleep! Sleep!
When thou tirest for thy home,
   Weary for thy rest,
Call love, and he shall come,
   And bear thee to his breast.
    So it is best.

MARY ROBINSON.

WHEN THE SUMMER DAYS
ARE DONE.

WHEN the summer days are done,
  And the sere leaves one by one
    Dust to dust are falling,
Patter, patter on the ground,
In the woodland glades around
You may hear the doleful sound
  Of their perpetual falling ;
Falling, falling night and day
Into darkness and decay ;
While from withering branch and stem,
Drop by drop in grief for them,
  The pearly dews are falling.

When the summer days are done,
And the shadows one by one
  Over earth are creeping,
Shadows of November gloom,
Shadows of the pale flowers' doom,
Gathered in untimely tomb,
  O'er the bleak hills creeping ;
Clammy fingers of decay
Close around us night and day,
And athwart the dreary dale,
Shrilly sounds the piercing gale
  Of winter nearer creeping.
                    J. H. DAVIES.

CHRYSANTHEMUMS.

WHEN Summer flowers have passed
    away—
    Each lingering petal shed,
When Nature dons a sober grey,
    And the last rose is dead ;
When trees have lost their robes of green—
    Then, like a regal dower,
The glad chrysanthemum is seen—
    Old Autumn's fairest flower.

So, too, when health and strength grow less,
    And age is creeping on ;
When Summer's joy and happiness
    Have blossomed and have gone—
Then, in the Autumn of our days,
    Bright precious blooms appear :
New hopes, new joys, to grace the ways
    Of life's swift-closing year.

GRIEVING.

SHE sat and watched the light of day
   Over the blue hills fading slow,
   And listened to the wind that wailed
     In crooning voice of long ago.

The fire upon the hearth burned dim ;
   Out came night-shadows weird and wild ;
And dead leaves swept across the path,
   Where once the blooming roses smiled.

No word she spake, but silent sat
   As white and still as sculptured stone ;
The living, breathing world around
   A sepulchre had sudden grown,

In which her buried life was laid,
   And over-writ this epitaph :
" Alas ! how soon man's fondest hopes
   Are scattered to the wind as chaff."

The clouds rolled o'er the misty moon ;
   In gentle sobs the raindrops spoke ;
Fell drop by drop the maiden's tears ;
   And answering sobs the stillness broke.

And through the wakening throbs of pain
   She found the living world once more ;
But sun and moon and stars had changed,
   And shone upon a foreign shore.

Life's river ebbed in turbid waves,
   That late had sparkled at her feet ;
A jarred note rang through every chord
   That until now had sounded sweet ;

And in a darkened world her steps
     Must wander, till her weary
      soul,
    Through sorrow gaining
      strength, shall win
     For her a fadeless aureole.
      JULIA GODDARD.

UNDER THE MISTLETOE.

YEARS ago I loved a maiden
    With a boy's love pure and true ;
  We as children played together,
    Grief and joy in common knew ;
And my love was bright and winsome,
  Dearer than all else to me,
Merry face with sunshine smiling,
Roguish eyes poor me beguiling—
    Laughter-loving Rosalie !

Years fled by, and one dark winter
    Cast a shadow o'er our joy,
For it brought a day of parting,
    When I was no more a boy ;
And my heart with grief was heavy
  But my child-love shed no tears,
Only leading where close-twining
Mistletoe above was shining,
    There she kissed away my fears.

Once again to home returning
  After many a struggling year,
Stand I 'neath the well-known portal
  Half in hope and half in fear.
What! is this shy blushing maiden
  She I left long years ago—
She who led me smiling brightly,
Lifted up her young face lightly,
  Kissed me 'neath the mistletoe?

What is this her arms encircle?
  Mistletoe and holly bright!
Omen this that seems to tell me
  She has ne'er forgot that night!
So, with glad hope strong within me,
  To her side I softly go.
Pluck a green twig from her slily,
Lift her sweet face blushing shyly,
  Kiss her 'neath the mistletoe.   G. W.

CONFESSION.

Y love is like a rose that grows
  Low down, and hid where no one knows ;
A rose that blossoms on the tree
Where those that look will never see.

My love is like a star at night
  Among a thousand stars of light ;
A single star that shines for me,
When those who look will never see.

And like the star, and like the rose,
My love is mine and no one knows ;
And bright with light and beauty, she
Is sweet alone, and sweet for me.

A REFLECTION.

FROM yon high shore
   The cedar that salutes the morning sun,
   And views some vessel far as sight can reach,
Whose sails have felt the tempest, and whose sides
Vibrated to remotest ocean's roar—
Reflects in some clear shallow by the beach
Its tufted roof of autumn gold, whereon

Sidelong the gentle sea-wind bends, and plays
Under its listening leafy ears, and soon
Returns with some fresh fancy, which the rays
Upon the simple surface mirror below ;
Until the western chasm grows blank, and slow
From the sad sea-line, murmurous with the flow
Of the night's rising tide, comes the calm moon.

T. C. IRWIN.

ERE THE NIGHT.

LOOK out across the waters
  To the gold and crimson west,
  Where the regal sun is drawing
  Evening's veil before his breast ;
Ere, with kindly care for mortals
  Who are weary and o'erworn,
He permits night's dusky portals
  To close o'er him until morn ;
And I gaze upon his glory
  Till I feel no more forlorn.

I had been o'ertried and driven
  Ere I brought my boat to shore,
For the wind had been untoward,
  And the current mocked my oar ;
But the baffling breeze tore past me,
  Cheering zephyrs glassed the tide,
And ere evening's shades o'ercast me
  I have touched the hither side,
And in yonder sunset glory
  I see hope re-typified.

ISABELLA BANKS.

THE LOVE-LETTER.

MAIDEN with the sunny eyes,
　In which the glad light's beaming,
While many a varying sunbeam flies
　Across thy bright face gleaming!
Why stand you on the old oak stair,
　While morning sunlight's glancing
On snowy breast and golden hair,
　And o'er thy rich dress dancing?

What do you there, with stealthy tread
　So slily onward gliding,
Half turning round in gleeful dread,
　The panelled oak back sliding?
What seek you in the wainscot there,
　Your little hand round creeping?
Take care, take care, O maiden fair,
　Lest some one should be peeping!

The glad light in your face tells plain
　You've found what you were seeking;
Then push the panel back again—
　Hark! hark! The old oak's creaking!
There's a step upon the stairs close by!
　Quick, now, O joyous maiden,
And far from danger swiftly fly,
　With Love's fond missive laden!

Ah, Love! you've been at work again—
　One never finds you sleeping;
And they will only watch in vain
　Who guard 'gainst thee are keeping!
But better so—for without thee
　All would in life grow weary;
Without the sun the changeless sea
　Would soon be sad and dreary!

THE CHILDREN OF THE TOWN.

WHEN summer suns are shining,
 And countless joys are ours—
The matchless grace of nature,
 The fragrance of the flowers—
When lingering by the ocean,
 Or on the heath-clad down,
What are our brothers doing—
 The children of the town?

In many a narrow alley,
 In many a crowded room,
They sit with pallid faces
 Amid the dirt and gloom !
They've never seen a daisy,
 Or heard a rippling stream ;
Speak to them of the ocean—
 They count it but a dream !

When we ourselves are happy,
　　'Tis easy to forget
The cheerless lives around us,
　　The work before us set !
Yet how enjoy the pleasures
　　That make up summer's crown,
While thousands of our brothers
　　Are pining in the town ?

Shame on us if we do it !
　　Shame on us all for aye !
Oh, surely we can give them
　　One summer holiday !
One glimpse of bounteous nature,
　　Of bird and flower and tree ;
One day of healthy breezes,
　　One day beside the sea.

　　　　　　　　　G. WEATHERLY.

61

SOME OTHER DAY.

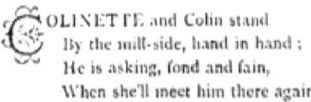 OLINETTE and Colin stand
By the mill-side, hand in hand ;
He is asking, fond and fain,
When she'll meet him there again ;

But vainly still to read he tries
Answer in her merry eyes :
Colinette will only say,
"Some other day ! Some other day ! "

Pleading with a lover's power
That she'll fix the very hour ;
But Colinette will only say,
"Some other day ! Some other day ! "

"Some other day, sweetheart," says he,
"Very far away may be ! "
"By the same rule, Colin dear,
It may be also very near ! "

Some other day came very soon—
Came, in fact, before next noon ;
Words forgot their fixed intent.
"Every day" her answer meant.
But, for love of golden days,
Colinette ne'er changed her phrase ;
At parting she would always say,
"Some other day ! Some other day ! "

F. E. WEATHERLY.

SCOOPED from a bed of living stone
  By glaciers' might when Time was young,
Ere man's intrusive step was known,
  A mystic beauty o'er thee hung,

Not seldom fanned by slumber's breath,
  In fairy lands, as morning sighed,
Entranced I saw the rose-hued heath
  Bend down to kiss thy playful tide ;

Sweet lake ! still sleep'st thou lucid, grand,
While those old mountains watchful stand.

Thy mimic waves I loved to cleave
  With eager arm, and lured thy trout ;
Or doth bewildering fancy weave
  Her spells my longing eyes to flout ?
How oft, too, 'mid thy sunset glow,
Idly my shallop's sail would blow !

And heard, across thy lonely moor
The dog bark by the shepherd's door.

Sleep, tranquil lake ! earth's troublous showers
  Disturb not thee ; thy far-spread gleam
Irradiates our working hours,
  And cheers us with a kindred dream.
Too happy if thy type we find
In sunny recollections shrined.

A SONG OF THE HARVEST.

'TIS harvest-tide, and a tremulous quiver
  Ripples across the broad seas of grain ;
  The breezes whisper the news to the river ;
    That harvest time has come again !
And the river, rapt in its secret, hushes,
Then carries its tale to the swaying rushes,

Who nod their heads in solemn pride ;
But the listening birds that round them throng
Break blithely forth in joyous song—
  " Hurrah for the ripe corn far and wide !
  Hurrah for the golden harvest-tide !"

At eventide glad earnest voices
  Unite in chorus pure and strong :
The weary son of toil rejoices,
  And the children join the harvest song :
Until when the ruddy sunset flushes
  Die out in the west, the chorus hushes,
And a chant of praise for wants supplied
  Goes up to Him who gives the grain ;
And then all hearts break forth again—
  " Thank God for the ripe corn far and wide !
  Thank God for the joyous harvest-tide ! "

SEPTEMBER WOODS.

A GLORY of gold
And russet and grey,
The tree-tops old
Glow in the day;
And, one by one,
The dry leaves fall,
And the Autumn sun
Smiles on them all.

Where all is still
The rabbits play,
And pheasants fill
Each woodland way;
And, one by one,
The dry leaves fall,
While the Autumn sun
Smiles on them all.

WHEN.

WHEN we were boys and girls together,
    Playing out amongst the gorse,
What thought we of wintry weather,
    Partings, changes, or remorse?
All before us bright and glowing,
    As we grouped upon the grass,
Telling tales of fortunes growing
    For each buoyant lad or lass:
Life was all a dream unbroken;
    Love a word unwrit, unspoken.

When we were boys and girls together,
    What thought we of worldly ways?
Never lambs amongst the heather
    Had less dread of stormy days;
Sun, and stream, and birds above us,
    Filled us with their warmth and life;
We loved all things, all things loved us,
    Nothing boded future strife,
When we spent our days together,
    Boys and girls 'mong gorse and heather.

ISABELLA BANKS.

THE HOUR OF REST.

BENEATH the green impleachèd trees,
  Beside the stream I pass :
I hear the bird upon the breeze,
  The breeze among the grass.
What is thy song, O breeze ? O bird ?
O sweet bird, flying to thy nest ?
    " Rest to the weary world,
      Rest ! rest ! "

Sleep soon, O world, thy rest is brief !
  Sink soon, thou westering beam !
The stream is singing to the leaf,
  The leaf unto the stream.
What is thy song, O leaf ? O stream ?
O grey stream flowing to the west ?
    " Rest to the weary world,
      Rest ! rest ! "   F. E. W.

A TEXT AMONG THE CRESSES.

STAR-LIKE honeysuckle trailing
　　O'er the fence in wreaths capricious,
　Summer breezes sailing, sailing,
　　Idly by with breath delicious ;
And a merry falling tinkle,
　Where the brook sweeps mossy ledges,
And a sparkle, and a twinkle,
　Of the water 'neath the sedges.

And a merry little maiden,
　With her tangled golden tresses,

Standing barefoot there, all laden
　With a wealth of emerald cresses ;
With her white feet in the water,
　Oh, so fresh and cool and pleasant !
And the green boughs arched athwart her,
　In a swinging, swaying crescent.

And she sings, in rambling rhyming,
　Some child-lay of " Brown-haired Kitty,"
While the brook is chiming, chiming,
　With her sweet uneven ditty.

Little Nell, the blacksmith's daughter,
  Pet and pride of all the village,
Paddling in the tinkling water,
  Cresses from its breast to pillage.

But the artist, as he passes,
  List'ning to the baby measure,
Crushing down the scented grasses
  With his strong foot, looks with pleasure,
"Such a gem for sketch or painting!"
  Thinks he, as he gently pauses,
And the song, descending, fainting,
  Dies away in broken clauses.

Then the golden locks are shaken,
  And the treasured pebbles rattle,
And the sketch is duly taken,
  'Mid the lassie's mirth and prattle;
"Oh, who taught you? you are clever!"
  (Sweet unconscious little preacher),
"Will the picture last for ever?
  Shall you give it to your teacher?"

Fortune, fame, the smiles of fashion,
  Crown the artist with successes,
London ladies take a passion
  For the pictured child and cresses;
But he bows to Christ the Master,
  As he older grows, and richer,
Ever hears, as praise falls faster,
  "Shall you give it to your teacher?"

All true art from God proceedeth,
  Yield thy first-fruits to His honour;
For thy soul with light He feedeth,
  Showers loveliness upon her;
On this faith he reared his glory,
  And this brief text was his preacher,
Till he died, renowned and hoary—
  "Shall you give it to your teacher?"

                                    M. M. P.

SAILED TO-NIGHT.

VER the moonlit sea,
  Far away from Devon and me,
    My lover has sailed to-night !—
  And I may lie and weep,

Whilst my kindred are fast asleep,
  Such tears as are kept from sight—
Weep, till my eye grows dim
  Underneath the reddening rim,

70

For the love I drove away ;
Weep with an aching brain,
And a heart full of hidden pain,
    That must never see the day.

The love I could not tell
Lay deep in my heart as a well,
    Where I kept my secret hid ;
And when he came I know,
Though forehead and cheek were aglow,
    My lip was a closed lid.

I could not cry aloud
" I love you," for, oh, I was proud,
    As I thought a maid should be ;
So when he came to woo,

I bound up my roses with rue,—
    And *now*, he's off o'er the sea.

No wreck e'er cast ashore
'Mid the wind and the water's roar
    Could be such a wreck as I ;
Lost on the reefs of pride,
To be lashed by the chafing tide,
    Of memory till I die.

Yet haply, after years,
When I have out-wept youthful tears,
    My love may re-sweep the main :
And then if he come to sue,
He will find me tranquil, but true,
    And leave me never again.

ISABELLA BANKS.

THE REALMS OF THE DEEP.

SEA SONG.

ASTERN, the long white wake of foam
    Points backward to our island home,
    Ahead, the waste of waters wide
Is still before us, all untried ;
The merry ship a creature seems,
Alive and full of joyous dreams—
    Dreams such as true love keep,
    Dreams glad as childhood's sleep.
Then away with the breeze o'er the foaming seas,
    To the realms of the mighty deep.

Away, the West has purple seas,
Wherein are mirrored slender trees,
Which wave where man is ever free,
And no proud despot's rule may be ;
Where summer still eternal beams,
And islands blessed are full of dreams—
    Dreams such as flowers know,
    Dreams bright as sunset glow.
Then away with the breeze o'er the foaming seas,
    To the land of the West we go.

Away, the coral islands white
Are brilliant in the morning light ;
Smooth valleys rich with golden green,
Long curves of yellow sand between,
And misty snows of falling streams,

With towering mountains full of dreams—
　　Dreams sweet as mother's kiss,
　　Dreams filled with purest bliss.
Then away with the breeze o'er the foaming seas,
　　To the land which can promise this.

F. H. H.

IN A GARDEN.

WHO loves fair flowers,
    And shady bowers
And all the joys a garden brings,
    Knows sweet content
    And merriment
Far more than happiest of kings.

    The whispering trees,
    The murmuring bees,
Each flower that nods, each bird that sings,
    Are good friends sent
    With sweet content
Unknown to happiest of kings.

BLOSSOM AND FRUIT.

BLOSSOM, blossom, sweet and fair,
  Blossom, blossom, everywhere ;
  On the hill-side, in the dell :
What the fruit ? ah, who can tell ?

Blossom, blossom, sweet and fair,
Blossom, blossom, everywhere,
In the pride of youth and strength :
What the harvesting at length ?

Blossom, blossom, sweet and fair,
Blossom, blossom, everywhere,
In life's early summer-time :
What the fruit in manhood's prime ?

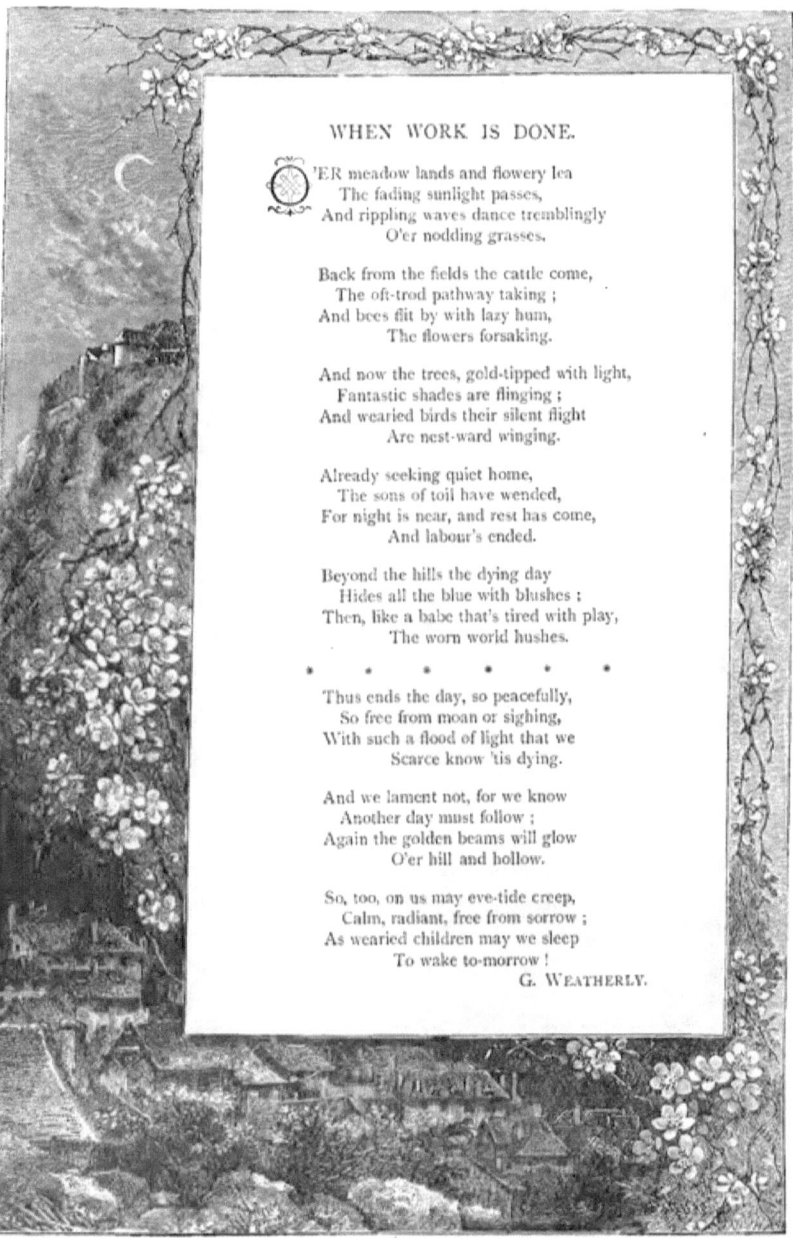

WHEN WORK IS DONE.

'ER meadow lands and flowery lea
  The fading sunlight passes,
And rippling waves dance tremblingly
    O'er nodding grasses.

Back from the fields the cattle come,
  The oft-trod pathway taking ;
And bees flit by with lazy hum,
    The flowers forsaking.

And now the trees, gold-tipped with light,
  Fantastic shades are flinging ;
And wearied birds their silent flight
    Are nest-ward winging.

Already seeking quiet home,
  The sons of toil have wended,
For night is near, and rest has come,
    And labour's ended.

Beyond the hills the dying day
  Hides all the blue with blushes ;
Then, like a babe that's tired with play,
    The worn world hushes.

*   *   *   *   *   *

Thus ends the day, so peacefully,
  So free from moan or sighing,
With such a flood of light that we
    Scarce know 'tis dying.

And we lament not, for we know
  Another day must follow ;
Again the golden beams will glow
    O'er hill and hollow.

So, too, on us may eve-tide creep,
  Calm, radiant, free from sorrow ;
As wearied children may we sleep
    To wake to-morrow !

G. WEATHERLY.

TWO HOMES.

I KNOW a little leafy bower
   Where may and blackthorn are in
      flower,
And, there, half hid from sight,
Two little birds have made their nest,
And, sun or shade, content they rest,
  And think the whole world bright.

I know a little cottage home,
Where sweetest of sweet roses roam,
  And there, half hid from sight,
Two loving hearts have made their nest,
And, sun or shade, content they rest,
  And think the whole world bright.

LONG AGO.

THE golden sunset's last faint ray
    Has faded out of sight ;
'Midst lingering shadows of the day,
    Comes on the wintry night ;

And sitting by the fire-light's glow,
    I watch the ruddy blaze,
And muse on all the long-ago,
    The happy by-gone days.

The past events of early youth,
    Fond childhood's grief and glee,
Shine forth again with vivid truth,
    Painted by Memory.
I seem to pass through life again,
    To feel its hopes and fears,
To taste once more the joy and pain
    Of well-nigh seventy years.

And as I watch the blazing glow,
    I see myself stand there,
Just as I was long years ago,
    When I was young and fair :

When *one* had whispered of his love.
  And blushes rosy-red
Told plainly any words above
  The words I left unsaid.

And then a happy joyous time
  Gleams forth from out the fire,
And fancy weaves a merry chime
  From a far-distant spire—
A merry chime of wedding-bells
  That floated on the breeze,
And made sweet music in the dells,
  And whispered to the trees.

Since then full many and many a year
  Has swiftly passed away,
With many a sorrow, many a tear,
  And many a cloudy day ;
And yet life's joyous sunny gleams
  Have oft shone golden-bright,
And summer morning's gladd'ning beams
  Have followed each dark night.

Ah, every scene of long-past days!
  I see you all once more,
In the fitful fire-light's dancing blaze,
  In the shadows on the floor !

Oh, memories, fond and sweet to me !
  I hold you very dear,
Like the notes of some soft melody
  Heard in a by-gone year !

C. W.

THE KING OF HEARTS.

S WIFTER than the swiftest eagle
    Striking surely great and small,
      Cometh Love, the mighty master,
        Cometh Love to one and all !
Lightning flashes linger o'er him,
All must bend and bow before him—
Love the tyrant, the oppressor,
    Love, the king the wide world o'er,
Love that holds us, and enfolds us
      In his grasp for evermore !

Suddenly, without a warning,
    Like a sunbeam through the shade,
Flasheth Love through hearts of mortals,
    Cometh Love to youth and maid !
None have any power o'er him,
Proud and lowly bend before him—
Love, the ever-welcome tyrant,
    Binding hearts the wide-world o'er ;
Love that braves us and enslaves us,
      Love the king for evermore !